Flying
Solo

MERIDIAN®

Flying Solo

Barbara **KESEL**
WRITER

Joshua **MIDDLETON**
PENCILER

Dexter **VINES**
INKER

Michael **ATIYEH**
COLORIST

CHAPTER 5
Paul **MOUNTS**
GUEST COLORIST

CHRONICLES 1.5
George **PÉREZ**
PENCILER
Mike **PERKINS**
INKER
Laura **DEPUY**
COLORIST

CHAPTER 6
Steve **MCNIVEN**
PENCILER
John **DELL**
INKER
Morry **HOLLOWELL**
COLORIST

CHAPTER 7
Steve **MCNIVEN**
PENCILER
Jordi **ENSIGN**
GUEST INKER
Morry **HOLLOWELL**
COLORIST

Dave **LANPHEAR** · LETTERER

CrossGeneration Comics   **Oldsmar, Florida**

Flying Solo

features Chapters 1 - 7
of the ongoing series
MERIDIAN

This place grows colder, my friend. Its energy wanes. I am seeking a solution, and eagerly welcome your thoughts.

It is not like you to be so troubled.

So long ago, when it was all set in motion, it was so... fascinating in its complexity. It surprised even me. Now things are static, worlds grow cold, and what were once glorious fields of battle lay still and barren.

The problem is not simply lazy warriors. The vital energies on which we all depend are fading away... it shouldn't happen like this... yet it is! It is dying, and the First do nothing to prevent it!

Because the First don't understand. They have no idea of the connection between their actions and the Whole.

Yes. They need...motivation. They must be forced to reignite the cycle...

Yet...they know nothing of my existence. To do so would *change* them...

Why look only to the First?

Chapter

1

THERE ARE MANY WORLDS OPEN TO YOU, SO MANY PEOPLE...

IF YOU WERE TO STEP IN QUIETLY -- WALK AMONG THEM. THEN A SUBTLE TOUCH, TO ADD JUST A SMALL MARK OF YOUR PASSAGE -- A SIGN.

YOUR SIGN.

IMAGINE... EACH WORLD. ONE SOUL, MARKED WITH THE SIGIL. OPENED TO THE POWER.

WHY JUST ONE?

I WAS THINKING IN TERMS OF EFFICIENCY. THE NUMBER IS UNIMPORTANT. A SMALL NUMBER MAKES FOR A CLEAR BURDEN ON EACH; TOO MANY, AND THEY LET SOMEONE ELSE DO THE WORK.

AS WE HAVE ALREADY SEEN WITH THE FIRST. STILL...

COME...

1.2

WHERE ARE WE?

ON THE EDGES OF
THE BLEAK ZONE. THE
VERY SPOT WHERE
IT ALL SEEMS TO DIE
AWAY. THIS WORLD
ITSELF IS A THING OF
RARE BEAUTY RAVAGED
BY THE CHANGES OF
TIME, A PEARL
DELICATELY POISED
ON THE EDGE
OF AN ABYSS.

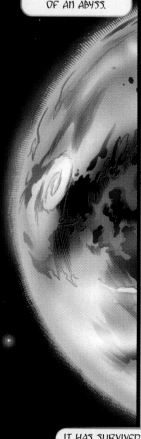

IT HAS SURVIVED
ONE CATACLYSM
AND ITS PEOPLE
THRIVE IN THE
RESULTING SKY
CITIES, MANAGING
A TENDER BALANCE
BETWEEN THE
RESOURCES
AVAILABLE TO
THEM AND THEIR
OWN DESIRE TO
POSSESS MORE.

A SINGLE SIGIL-BEARER WOULD DISRUPT THAT BALANCE. *TWO* WOULD PRESERVE THE TENSION...

TWO SIBLINGS, this time... I think...

WHAT WILL I tell them, these... *SIGIL-BEARERS?*

GIVE THEM NO WARNING, NO DIRECTION; LET THEIR ACTIONS DICTATE THE FLARE OF THE SIGIL.

THIS WILL REENERGIZE YOUR WARRIORS. BRING THEM BACK TO THEIR PURPOSE. HAVE THEM FIGHT OFF THE CHILL OF THEIR CURRENT ENNUI.

You mean CROSS-GENERATION.

YES, POWER FROM CONFLICT. ENERGY CREATING ENERGY.

AS THE NEW ONES WORK TOWARD THEIR OWN DEFINITION, THEY SERVE YOUR NEEDS.

I TELL YOU, YOU COULD START A NEW CHAIN OF CREATION TO STOKE THE COOLING FIRES OF THE WHOLE.

I FEEL IT GROWING WARMER ALREADY.

Little memories. My house.

My room...

...my freedom...

HI, FEABIE! HI, ZOUKA!

I'M HOME!

LATE AGAIN...

...SUCH A SURPRISE!

SEPHIE, YOU'RE AS CONSTANT AS THE STARS...

...WE HAVE TO STAY UP LATE TO SEE *THEM*, TOO!

SHE KNEW MINISTER ILAHN WAS VISITING TODAY...

...BUT SHE JUST HAD TO SEE *JAD.*

DID *NOT!*

IS HE HERE YET, MIRA?

RIGHT OUTSIDE.

MY LORD MINISTER...!

...PRESENTING **ILAHN,** MINISTER OF CADADOR!

STOP BARKING LIKE AN OVER-ZEALOUS HERALD, REGOR. THEY KNOW WHO I AM.

ILAHN! HOW FARES THE LAND OF CADADOR?

TUROS... MY ARM.

FORGIVE ME MY EXUBERANCE, ILAHN -- MY PRIDE IS OVERFLOWING!

JUST LOOK AT OUR SEPHIE TODAY!

GREETINGS, UNCLE.

COME -- LET US STEAL A LITTLE TIME ALONE BEFORE I LOSE YOU TO TABLE TALK!

1.12

Ah... *QUAINT* AS EVER.

TUROS... I'LL NEVER UNDERSTAND... MERIDIAN IS WEALTHY ENOUGH...

WHY CAN'T YOU RAZE THESE HOVELS AND BUILD SOMETHING MAGNIFICENT?

NOT EVERYONE HAS A TASTE FOR GILT AND ORNAMENT, ILAHN. THERE'S BEAUTY IN SIMPLICITY --

HAVE YOU FORGOTTEN THE VIEW FROM THE MOUNTAINS?

I'VE BECOME A CIVILIZED MAN, BROTHER -- ROCKS AND DIRT ARE FOR CHILDREN AND PEASANTS.

I APPRECIATE THE ART OF BRILLIANT MINDS, NOT MINDLESS NATURE.

WE MUST AGREE TO DISAGREE, THEN, ILAHN. TO YOUR HEALTH.

AND YOURS. I'VE HEARD YOU ARE... UNWELL?

I'VE KEPT IT QUIET. MY PHYSICIANS CAN'T FIND A CAUSE.

IN HONESTY, BROTHER -- I'M AFRAID, BUT I'M NOT WILLING TO SEND MY ASHES TO THE WIND JUST YET.

GIVEN YOUR CONCERNS, PERHAPS YOU'LL RECONSIDER MY OFFER TO COMBINE MERIDIAN AND CADADOR?

THE PEOPLE OF MERIDIAN ARE TOO DIFFERENT FROM YOURS IN CAPADOR. WE ARE CRAFTSMEN, NOT MERCHANTS.

IT MIGHT BE GOOD FOR OUR PURSES, BUT IT WOULDN'T BE GOOD FOR OUR SOULS.

I MUST DECLINE, ILAHN. AGAIN AND ALWAYS.

STARS BURN YOUR STUBBORN HIDE! *THINK*, TUROS!

IS A PASSIVE, BACKWARD STATE A FITTING LEGACY FOR YOUR CHILD? THIS SHORT-SIGHTEDNESS OF YOURS IS COSTING US BOTH!

I WON'T ALLOW IT!

YOU ARE FORCING ME TO ACKKK

GET AWAY!

STOP! IT'S JUST A--

--BIRD?

If Papa hadn't been so sick, everything could have been so different...

As it was,
Papa was weak.

When it
happened...

...whatever it was
that did happen...

GYAAUGH!

...it was
just too
much.

AAAK--

TUROS?
THAT
CREATURE --
WHAT HAS IT
DONE?!

TUROS?

PAPA?

In my dreams that night, there was this strange feeling... I had to find something... someone?

There was a connection between this thing? person? and my father and me.

I had to hunt it down FAST or lose something precious.

As I turned to follow it...

...there was a
BLINDING light.

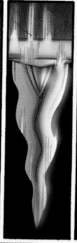

It exploded
right at me...

...then it flowed through me.
I was filled with its warmth...
suddenly, I felt protected.

I woke up realizing
I was, somehow, safe.

1.24

SUCH A WONDERFUL PLACE. WHAT A PITY.

HASTIAN -- STILL NO SIGN OF SEPHIE?

NO, MA'AM.

WE'VE BEEN THROUGH THE ENTIRE PLACE.

SHE MIGHT BE OUT COLD SOMEWHERE, BUT NO ONE'S SEEN HER.

DID SEPHIE GET BURNED, HASTIAN?

SEPHIE WASN'T IN THE FIRE, JORGY...

WE DON'T KNOW WHERE SHE WENT, BUT SHE'S SAFE.

NO TUROS, NO SEPHIE... NO HOUSE ON THE HILL...

IT'S LIKE THE HEART'S BEEN TORN FROM MERIDIAN.

STILL AWAKE?

YOU SHOULD TRY TO SLEEP, CHILD.

THIS DAY HAS BEEN DOUBLY TRAGIC, BUT IT'S OVER. YOU'RE SAFE.

REST NOW...

"...TOMORROW WE CAN BEGIN TO PLOT MERIDIAN'S COURSE..."

"...TOGETHER."

SO MUCH HAS CHANGED JUST IN ONE DAY I HARDLY RECOGNIZE MYSELF ANYMORE. EVERYTHING'S NEW...

...AND *STRANGE.*

WHATEVER IT IS WONT EVEN COME OFF.

WHY CAN'T THE WORLD BE THE WAY IT USED TO—

AAH!

SEPHIE...

...WE SHOULD TALK.

UNCLE ILAHN! I... I DIDN'T HEAR YOU COME IN.

OF COURSE. WE'LL TOUR CAPADOR PROPER TOMORROW.

I HAVEN'T HAD THE CHANCE TO THANK YOU FOR... BRINGING ME TO YOUR ESTATE.

SEPHIE, I NEED TO SHOW YOU SOME-THING.

WE'VE BOTH BEEN MARKED.

BUT IT'S NOT YET SAFE TO REVEAL OUR SELVES. YOUR LIFE MA DEPEND UPON KEEPIN YOUR GIFT A SECRET.

YOU AS WELL? DO YOU HAVE ANY IDEA WHAT THEY MEAN?

THEY'RE MARKS OF GREATNESS. OF POWER.

THIS IS FOR YOU.

THANK YOU, IT'S... PRETTY.

THE SORT OF THING YOUR MOTHER WOULD'VE WORN, I THINK. I WANT YOU TO USE IT TO *HIDE* THE MARK YOU BEAR.

IF PEOPLE KNEW WHAT WE COULD DO...

...WELL, IT'S JUST BETTER THEY *DON'T.*

REMEMBER, SEPHIE, OUR SECRET. A *FAMILY* SECRET.

I UNDERSTAND, UNCLE ILAHN.

GOOD NIGHT.

MERIDIAN • CHAPTER TWO

On Meridian, we kept true to the old ways...

Other cities rushed to grow, adding ore pods to their bottoms so they could add mass topside...

...but we preferred to keep things in balance.

"When need and want in balance rest, tension is barred And work is best."

2.1

It was always so peaceful there.

2.2

Cadador, on the other hand...

...wore peace like a beautiful robe-- hiding its weapons inside the folds.

DID YOU HEAR? CADADORIAN TROOPS

INVASION FORCE

MERIDIAN'S BEEN TAKEN OVER!

WE'RE INVADING MERIDIAN?

WHAT? ARE THEY TALKING ABOUT MERIDIAN?

STREET TALK. DON'T TROUBLE YOURSELF WITH RUMORS, SEPHIE.

OVER A THOUSAND TROOPERS

AT LAST! MORE ROOM

BURNED TO THE GROUND

BUT IF SOMETHING HAS HAPPENED...!

FIVE SHIPLOADS OF MEN

ABOUT TIME WE SOLVED THE PROBLEM

PAPA ALWAYS SAID I HAVE A RESPONSIBILITY TO MERIDIAN FIRST!

I HAVE TO GO HOME.

HOME? RESP--

YOU *DO* HAVE A RESPONSIBILITY TO MERIDIAN. TO STAY HERE IN CADADOR.

TO *LEARN*. TO *GROW*. TO BECOME A *GREAT* MINISTER.

IF YOU GO HOME NOW, YOU PUT MERIDIAN IN THE HANDS OF AN AMATEUR...

...A MINISTER UNSCHOOLED IN THE TRICKS OF TRADE...

IS THAT THE *RESPONSIBLE* THING TO DO?

NO.

YOU'RE LEARNING ALREADY. GOOD GIRL.

HERE'S WHAT WILL HAPPEN. YOU REMAIN MINISTER IN EXILE...

NO, NO, NO, NO--!

SEPHIE!

FASTER! HE'S GOING TO GET AWAY!

INTO THE FIRE? CAN HE FLY?

Uh-oh.

JAD...

...OVER HERE!

FRISHA? AREN'T YOU SURROUNDED?

THE DOORS ARE BARRED -- WE HAVE THE *OTHER* ROADS OPEN!

HURRY!

Oh, DAD *TOLD* ME ABOUT THOSE!

I CAN'T BELIEVE IT --

--I'LL ACTUALLY HAVE A CHANCE TO USE THEM!

"SO IT'S *TRUE?*"

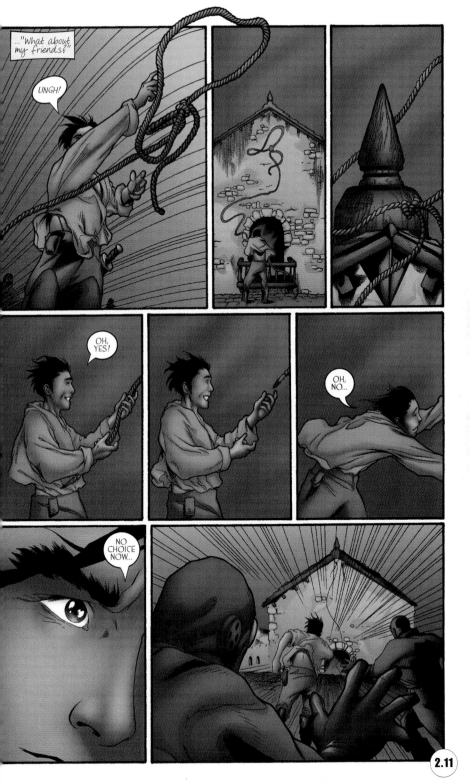

"...IT'S NOT LIKE THERE'S ANY SHADOWS TO HIDE IN!"

...TO GUARANTEE MERIDIAN AS PROSPEROUS AND SUCCESSFUL A FUTURE AS CADADOR!

STRONG SPEECH FROM THE MOUTH OF A MAN WHO WOULD PLANT THE KISS OF DEATH ON HIS OWN BROTHER'S LIPS!

SHE... KNOWS?

WHO ARE YOU, CREATURE?

I AM THE ONE WHO SEES WHAT IS TO COME...

...TWO SIDES IN OPPOSITION, NEVER TO TOUCH...

...I SEE YOUR SIGIL, EVEN THOUGH YOU HIDE ITS OUTER ASPECT...

YOU... SEE--?

I-- I--

BOSCAU!

HAVE THAT...WOMAN BROUGHT TO MY STUDY.

HAVE HER CLEANED FIRST.

FAREWELL, MY FRIENDS!

OUR PLAN IS IN MOTION, AND I'M OFF TO HOME!

BUT **WHY?**

ALL I WANT IS A LITTLE FRESH AIR!

WHY CAN'T I GO OUT?

YOUNG GIRLS SHOULDN'T BE SEEN AFTER SUNSET...

...IT SIMPLY ISN'T DONE.

WELL, I'M NOT STAYING LOCKED UP IN HERE! I'M NOT A PRISONER--

--I'M THE MINISTER OF MERIDIAN!

AND THE MINISTER SHOULD PREPARE TO RETIRE FOR THE DAY.

THE CITY STREETS ARE NOT SAFE FOR HER.

BUT...

BUT...

"--I HAVE *OTHER* DUTIES TO ATTEND TO, ANYWAY!"

NOK NOK

ENTER!

THE MINISTER OF CADADOR REQUESTED AN AUDIENCE WITH THIS... WOMAN?

I DID. SEE HER IN.

WE... DID OUR BEST, BUT...

YOU WISHED THEM TO CHANGE ME, BUT I WILL NOT BE CHANGED.

I AM WHAT I CHOSE TO BE.

YOU HAVE CHANGED.

Hmmm, I SEE -- YOU CALLED HER *HEARTSTEALER*, THEN--

SILENCE!

PLEASE EXCUSE US.

LEAVE!

WHO ARE YOU...

2.17

...because they'd barred the doors...

Escape was really a simple thing...

...but never thought about the windows.

Girls from Meridian aren't tied to the ground like the ones here.

I'd only been to Cadador on official family business...

...if I was going to live there, I had to know what it was really like.

Ilahn rules Cadador, but won't live on its land. He has his own island tethered at its side.

He doesn't really KNOW his city...

I know every inch of Meridian.

All around me, busy people filled the night with conversation, not shy about sharing their concerns... never noticing me.

Without the pronouncement of my title, I was invisible, just passing by like a ghost.

A ghost HEARING horrors, not causing them...

...I heard how these people, the lowsiders, weren't treated as well as those above...

How the people who lived below the horizon were thought of as less important than others of their SAME CITY...

How these people HATED my uncle for reinforcing the divisions of class.

And all the things they said he did...

A good Minister, they all said...

...but not a good man.

I always knew he wasn't as good a man as my father, but I hadn't had a chance to NOTICE what I'd been seeing...

Uncle Ilahn WASN'T a good man...

...and now he was in control of Meridian...

Oh, PAPA, I KNOW WHAT YOU'D SAY...

"LIFE HAS TOSSED YOU A TWIST -- TRY TO BEND WITH IT."

BUT THIS PLACE...

...IT JUST ISN'T... HOME.

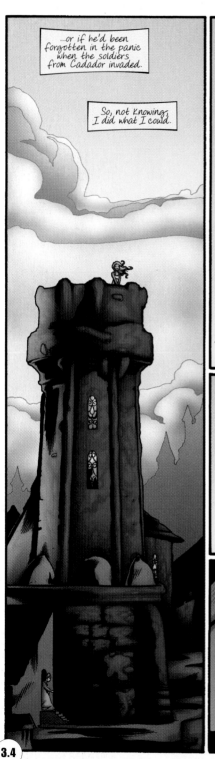

...or if he'd been forgotten in the panic when the soldiers from Cadador invaded.

So, not knowing, I did what I could.

GOODBYE, PAPA.

GOOD JOURNEY.

AAIEEE!

YES, ISRE?

CHILD, HAVE YOU LOST YOUR MIND? COME DOWN FROM THERE!

MINISTER ILAHN REQUESTS YOUR PRESENCE...

3.6

WHAT'S WRONG? YOUR ESCAPE WENT PERFECTLY, AND THAT *RESCUE*...

NOTHING'S WRONG.

YOU THINK *SEPHIE* SAW THAT?

SO... JUST WHERE *IS* SHE?

WE DON'T KNOW, JAD.

WE THINK SHE MAY HAVE GONE WITH ILAHN.

WHA--?

TO CADADOR?

SHE'D NEVER-- MIRA, I'VE GOT TO GO GET HER BACK!

JAD, *NO!*

WE JUST KEPT YOU OUT OF THE HANDS OF THE CADADORIAN SOLDIERS! DON'T GO RUSHING BACK IN!

DON'T YOU TELL ME WHAT TO DO! YOU'RE NOT MY MOTHER!

JAD!

FEABIE...

WHAT IS IT, JORGY?

ARE THE SOLDIERS GOING TO GET US LIKE THEY GOT SEPHIE?

Oh, DON'T YOU WORRY, SWEETIE...

...THEY WON'T FIND US HERE!

THE GROWNUPS HAVE TO PACK UP AND SET TRAPS...

...AND THEN WE'LL ALL RIDE ON A SHIP!

LET'S PLAY A GAME...

...WE'LL LOOK FOR SEPHIE ON OUR WAY!

BUT I CAN'T PLAY! I DON'T REMEMBER WHAT SHE LOOKS LIKE!

YOU'LL ALWAYS BE ABLE TO RECOGNIZE SEPHIE BECAUSE SHE HAS A MARK ON HER HEAD, RIGHT HERE!

DO YOU KNOW THE STORY? IT APPEARED MYSTERIOUSLY...

MORE MYSTERIES! YOU *PLAGUE* ME, MUSE...

..WE'VE BEEN AT THIS FOR TOO MANY HOURS NOW.

YOU GIVE ME OBSCURITIES AND HINTS WHEN I'M ASKING FOR *INFORMATION!*

THE EYES OF THE MUSE OF GIATAN SEE MANY THINGS. THE EYES OF THE MINISTER OF CADADOR ARE CLOUDED WITH NEED...

YES, I *NEED!*

I NEED TO *KNOW* IF THIS ABILITY IS A FUNCTION OF MY OWN NATURE...

...OR IF THE POWER I NOW POSSESS IS DUPLICATED IN MY NIECE!

UNCLE ILAHN?

THEY SAID...

COVER YOURSELF!

YOU SEE THE ANSWER, BUT YOU DO NOT KNOW IT...

PRESENTING THE REPRESENTATIVE FROM TORBEL, *SOLICITOR TRUPERT.*

SO RUDY SENT HIS BULLDOG, AND DIDN'T COME HIMSELF.

WATCH CLOSELY, SEPHIE-- MINISTER RUDEF MISTAKENLY BELIEVES HIMSELF TO HAVE THE UPPER HAND.

THIS HAS LED HIM TO ADOPT A DANGEROUSLY CASUAL APPROACH TO OUR NEGOTIATIONS.

MINISTER ILAHN! MINISTER RUDEF SENDS GREETINGS FROM TORBEL.

IT'S PAST TIME TO RENEW OUR ORE SUPPLY AGREEMENT.

SINCE WE DIDN'T RECEIVE A COURIER FROM CADADOR AND OUR SUPPLY IS RUNNING SHORT, HE SENT ME TO FINALIZE THE DEAL.

THERE'S A SMALL PROBLEM, I'M AFRAID.

TORBEL HAS *CHEATED* CADADOR.

YOU HAVE DELIVERED ORE VATS THAT I KNOW TO BE INFERIOR TO THOSE OF YOUR NEWEST PRODUCTION RUN.

CHEATED?

THERE'S NO CHEAT INVOLVED!

WE CONTACTED YOU, ILAHN. YOU WERE MADE AWARE THAT OUR MASTER IRONWORKERS HAD DESIGNED NEW, MORE EFFICIENT AND MORE EXPENSIVE ORE VATS!

YOU DIDN'T WANT TO PAY MORE, SO WE SUPPLIED VATS OF THE CONTRACTED STYLE AT THE CONTRACTED PRICE!

3.12

BUT I HAVE REVIEWED OUR CONTRACT. IT SPECIFIES THAT CADADOR WILL RECEIVE THE *FINEST AVAILABLE*.

YOU DRAFTED AND SIGNED AN AGREEMENT WITH THAT PROVISION INCLUDED.

THEREFORE, YOU SHOULD HAVE AUTOMATICALLY SHIPPED THE BETTER VATS.

THAT'S SALES PUFFERY, ILAHN!

THAT LANGUAGE ISN'T IN THE BODY OF THE CONTRACT -- I WON'T LET YOU PLAY A GAME OF WEASEL WORDS HERE!

STARS ABOVE, MAN -- YOU'RE WITHHOLDING ORE, PUTTING TORBEL IN JEOPARDY OVER A CASUAL PHRASE!

I'M NOT WITHHOLDING ORE. WE HAVE NO CURRENT CONTRACT FOR SUPPLY.

AND I DON'T MAKE *NEW* BUSINESS WITH THOSE WHO DO NOT KEEP THEIR WORD.

WE'RE FINISHED HERE. SEE THE MAN TO THE DOOR, BOSCAU.

BUT--

BUT--

ILAHN, DO YOU KNOW WHAT YOU'RE DOING?

TORBEL IS *MASSIVE*.

WITHOUT THAT ORE TO KEEP US ALOFT, TORBEL WILL *FALL!*

MINISTER ILAHN HAS CONCLUDED YOUR MEETING, SIR.

3.13

When Father did business, no one left the table until both sides were satisfied.

He wouldn't leave another city in danger.

Of course, we built ships on Meridian. No one would die if you refused to sell them a ship.

NOW, SEPHIE... WHAT DID YOU LEARN HERE?

It hurt me to realize Uncle Ilahn was willing to make good on his threat...

...all because of their attitude at the table...

...and a few miswritten words.

THAT PEOPLE SHOULD ALWAYS MAKE SURE THEY KEEP TO THE LETTER OF AN AGREEMENT, NOT JUST ITS INTENT.

PERCEPTION OF INTENT.

IF INTENT IS NOT CLEARLY OUTLINED IN THE LANGUAGE OF A CONTRACT, IT CANNOT BE USED AS AN EXCUSE FOR NON-PERFORMANCE OF SPECIFIED DUTIES.

BUT I HEARD...

A LOT OF PEOPLE IN CADADOR DON'T FAVOR A HOSTILE RELATIONSHIP WITH OTHER CITES.

WHERE DID YOU HEAR THAT?

Ah... AROUND.

WOULD YOU REALLY LET TORBEL FALL?

ONLY IF NECESSARY...

3.17

There was some good in Cadador's business.

Wealth made the city a great benefactor of artists.

I missed Meridian and Papa, but the pleasing result of one man's imagination made me feel a little more at home in this place that was so very...

...strange.

SO, YOU ARE BEGINNING TO SEE HIM MORE CLEARLY.

AAAH!

YOU SENSE THAT THE MEASURE OF YOUR FATHER'S BROTHER AS A MAN FALLS SHORT.

YOU EVEN BEGIN TO FEAR HIM...

I DIDN'T -- WHAT MAKES YOU SAY THAT?

I AM THE EYES.

I CANNOT HELP BUT SEE THE SECRETS.

ASK HIM, CHILD.

ASK HIM WHY HE KEEPS COLD ECHOING MEMORIES CLUTCHED INSIDE.

ASK HIM WHY THE PORTRAIT HE WEARS CLOSE TO HIS HEART BEARS YOUR MOTHER'S LIKENESS.

MY MOTHER?

I-- I'LL ASK HIM... NOW!

EX-EXCUSE ME...THANK YOU!

3.19

When I left Cadador that day...

...I not only left behind my only living relative...

...I left behind my first true enemy.

But I didn't care.

After all, I was the Daughter of Meridian...

...and I was going home.

THERE'S ONE.

ARN...!

NOW!

ONE, YOU SAY.

YOU *SURE?*

STAY BACK OUT OF SIGHT.

THE SUN'S PICKLED THAT OLD SAILOR'S BRAIN OF YOURS, JON --

-- DO YOU THINK I'M A BOY?

I REMEMBER THE MERCHANTS' WAR, TOO.

FPLF

I ALSO REMEMBER HOW TO LURE RATS.

GIVE A WHISTLE BEFORE I SNEEZE AGAIN.

WHEEET

FFFTT

WHAT'S GOING ON IN THERE?

HAH CHOO!

KWHACK

WHAT HAPPENED TO THE PARTY I WAS LEADING UP THE HILLS?

ALREADY DOWN THE CENTER ROAD. THEY'RE HALFWAY TO BEACON NOTCH BY NOW. ONE MORE STOP AND WE'RE NEXT.

THAT'S COMFORTING.

I QUESTIONED TUROS' WISDOM WHEN HE DECIDED TO EXPAND THE MAZE, BUT IT'S CERTAINLY A BOON TO US NOW.

THERE'S AN ACCESS NEARBY?

UNDER YOUR NOSE.

ME, I'VE SPENT THE LAST DECADE MAPPING AND EXPANDING THE TUNNELS WHILE *SOME* PEOPLE FLITTED AROUND ON BOATS...

...PROBABLY THE ONLY PERSON WHO KNOWS THESE PASSAGES AS WELL AS I DO IS *SEPHIE*...

KREEEEK

...THAT GIRL'S BEEN CURIOUS AS A CAT SINCE SHE COULD WALK!

I HOPE SHE'S WELL...

4.4

Racing away from Cadddor, I felt my heart leap for the first time since Papa died...

Home! Fair winds or foul, I was on my way...

...flying a ship that usually takes a crew of three, but I'd done that before.

The familiar, automatic actions left me free to think about everything that had happened.

I wasn't sure exactly how I'd stop an invasion by a whole army...

...but it had to be done.

I couldn't let Uncle Ilahn destroy Meridian.

I was Minister now. It was my job to protect...

...MERIDIAN?

Uncle Ilahn's estate...

...all my visits, and I'd never SEEN it.

I'd heard whispers of foolish construction...

...but no one ever told me he'd carved his little island into a copy of Meridian!

Maybe that's why Papa always berthed our ship on the other side?

It was horrible! All built-over like Cadador! No trees, no hills, only...palace!

Then it hit me... what I was looking at was a MODEL.

What Ilahn had sculpted there was what he intended to do to the real island!

AROOOWWWWWOOGAH

Not MY Meridian.

Not EVER.

Jad showed me a great stunt once.

It only works with the little airships.

You have to trick the wind into forcing you down against the ship's natural buoyancy.

You shift the ballast, set the sails to catch the shear, and hold on tight!

He calls it the "Death Dive."

You have to be very confident in your shiphandling abilities...

...and you can't be afraid to see the ground...

4.11

THANKS FOR YOUR HELP, NORY.

Oh, HA! LIKE TURNING A WINCH IS DANGEROUS LABOR!

I DID THE SAME FOR YOUR BOY, JON, GOING THE OTHER DIRECTION.

HE'S A FEARLESS ONE, THAT JAD.

YOU JUST RUSH BACK HERE ONCE YOU'VE GOT THE LAST ONES SO WE CAN ALL BE ON OUR WAY DOWN.

MY BARIA'S GONE AHEAD ALREADY...

TOO QUIET, JON-- AND FRISHA'S NOT IN SIGHT.

THEY'RE INSIDE.

GO BACK!

GO BACK DOWN! IT'S A TRAP!

NO, FRISHA--

-- WE WON'T LEAVE YOU, GIRL!

NO ONE WHO'S AGREED TO GO GETS LEFT BEHIND!

WHOMP

KRAAK

WHUMPF

IT'S BEEN A LONG TIME, BREHN.

I NEVER THOUGHT YOU'D COME BACK...

I DIDN'T. I'M JUST HERE AS A CADADORIAN SOLDIER.

YOU'D BETTER GET GOING...

...BUT SOMEBODY'S GOT TO HIT ME OR I'LL HAVE TOO MUCH TO EXPLAIN.

HAPPY TO OBLIGE.

YOU'RE WHERE YOU BELONG NOW, BOY--

--WITH CADADOR'S MERCENARIES!

DON'T CRY FOR HIM, LISELA.

THIS GOOD DEED DOESN'T REDEEM HIS TRANSGRESSIONS.

4.18

The Cadadorian soldiers were better sailors than I expected...

...I knew I was about to be caught.

LET'S COORDINATE THE SPEARS--

--WAIT ON MY *SIGNAL!*

But no one waited.

They were all afraid somebody else would get the credit...

As I tumbled, it was almost funny to watch it all twist around...

...you see, now, instead of fighting over who got the credit...

...it would be about who got the blame...

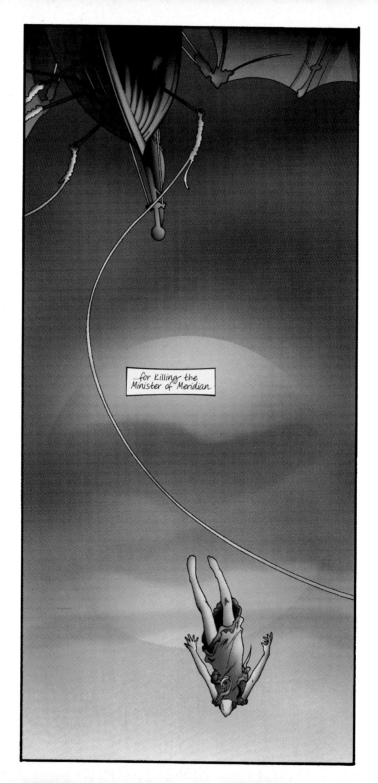

...for killing the
Minister of Meridian.

TORBEL, THE IRONWORKERS' CITY.

MINISTER ILAHN OF CADADOR SENDS HIS REGARDS AND THIS MESSAGE TO THE MINISTER OF TORBEL:

"SEPHIE, THE MINISTER OF MERIDIAN--"

VYLUND, WHERE LAWYERS ARE TAUGHT AND TESTED.

"-- HAS FLED MINISTER ILAHN'S CITY IN A FIT OF GRIEF.

"SHE IS YOUNG, AND HAS SUFFERED UNPRECEDENTED TRAGEDY..."

RING CITY, HOME OF BOOKBINDERS.

"...SO IS LIKELY HEADED HOME TO MERIDIAN.

"BUT TO MY FELLOW MINISTERS AND CLOSEST NEIGHBORS MAY I MAKE THIS SUGGESTION..."

NESCOAN, CITY OF CARRIAGEMAKERS.

"...RECEIVE HER COURTEOUSLY SHOULD SHE COME TO YOU.

"AND SEND A MESSENGER TO CADADOR IMMEDIATELY.

"SO I MAY ARRANGE FOR HER RETURN TO MY CARE."

In Meridian, the first story all children know is the tale about the monster called the Edge.

"Stay AWAY from the Edge."

"Children DIE at the Edge."

"You weren't playing near the EDGE?"

Every so often, a child is taken by the monster.

When we get older, we realize that although the Edge is real...

...the monster is just a tale to frighten children away from danger.

But although the monster doesn't exist...

...you suddenly understand the true danger of the edge...

...and you realize what happened to those children.

That's when the fear becomes REAL.

Then you grow up, and the Edge becomes just one more ordinary danger.

You don't think about the monster anymore.

At least, I didn't.

Until now.

The Monster had me.

I was going to join those lost children...

...so why wasn't I afraid?

5.4

MINISTER ILAHN?

HE'S STILL ASLEEP.

THE MINISTER WAS UP ALL LAST NIGHT INTERROGATING THAT GROTESQUE WOMAN.

THEN THAT WRETCHED NIECE OF HIS FLED...

...HE'S BEEN THROUGH ENOUGH FOR ONE DAY.

SEPHIE'S TRAGEDY WON'T CHANGE BEFORE MORNING.

BEST TO WAIT AND GIVE HIM THE NEWS ABOUT HER DEATH WHEN HE'S RESTED.

AYE. WE NEEDN'T ADD PAIN TO PAIN NOW.

Oh? IS IT HIS PAIN OR YOURS THAT CONCERNS YOU?

Uh...

...DAD?

DAD?

I --

--I'M SO SORRY, JAD --

-- BUT THERE JUST HADN'T BEEN A GOOD TIME TO TELL YOU...

Uh... OKAY.

BUT... YOU JUST *HAVEN'T*... NOT SINCE MOM...

YOUR MOTHER WOULDN'T BEGRUDGE ME A SECOND CHANCE--

I *KNOW*, PAD!

IT'S NOT *THAT!*

DID I HAVE TO FIND OUT *AFTER* EVERYBODY ELSE?

MIRA, *YOU* COULD HAVE LET ME KNOW...

BUT, JAD, YOU SAID IT YOURSELF...

...I'M NOT YOUR MOTHER.

ILAHN'S CASTLE...

...THE PRIDE OF CADADOR...

...MY NEW HOME.

NOK NOK

YESSSS?

GOOD MORNING!

I'D LIKE TO ARRANGE AN APPOINTMENT WITH MINISTER ILAHN.

YOU ARE CLEARLY THE MAJOR POMO OF HIS ESTATE.

I'M CERTAIN *YOU* COULD ARRANGE IT.

THERE ARE PROTOCOLS...

...WHICH ARE DESIGNED TO CONTROL THOSE WHO MINDLESSLY TAKE DIRECTION...

...NOT FOR INDEPENDENT THINKERS LIKE US.

CERTAINLY YOU COULD JUST SLIP ME IN ON HIS AGENDA...

Hmmmm....

COME BACK THIS AFTERNOON, I'LL SEE WHAT'S AVAILABLE.

LOROSI!

SSHHHH **KLEK**

YES, MY MINISTER?

SEND IN THE CAPTAIN.

I'M ANXIOUS TO HEAR WHAT CAPTAIN PATGIEN HAS TO SAY ABOUT WHY MY NIECE HAS NOT BEEN RETURNED TO ME.

YES, MY MINISTER.

STORM CLOUDS ON THE HORIZON.

5.11

MINISTER ILAHN.

WELCOME, CAPTAIN PATGIEN!

COME IN.

PLEASE, SIT DOWN.

EXPLAIN YOUR *TARDY* RETURN TO ME.

MAKE IT GOOD.

IN SHORT... WE *FAILED*, MY MINISTER.

THE MINISTER OF MERIDIAN'S SHIP WAS SPEARED...

...BUT SHE WAS NOT SECURED TO IT.

WE WERE UNABLE TO STOP HER.

SHE... FELL.

YOU'RE TELLING ME SHE'S... *DEAD?!*

BOSCAU, LOROSI...

...MY INTERVIEW WITH THE CAPTAIN IS OVER...

GNNNH!

...CLEAN UP THE MESS.

Oh, IDERIA...

...FORGIVE ME.

I'VE DESTROYED THE LAST OF YOU...

...STUPID, STUBBORN GIRL...

"..WHAT'S HAVING MERIDIAN WITHOUT YOU?"

IS THAT THE LAST OF THEM?

THE VERY LAST.

WHEN WE RETURN, IT WILL BE TO STAY.

NOW ALL THAT'S LEFT IS TO BOARD OUR PEOPLE AND LEAVE HOME.

THROUGH THAT GAPING HOLE THOSE CADADORS HAVE LEFT IN WHAT THEY PITIFULLY CALL SECURITY.

WE'D HAVE DONE BETTER.

STILL, I DON'T SEE WHY WE DON'T TAKE THEM ON NOW--

--I'M TOO OLD FOR THIS LEAVE-TAKING GAMBIT!

WHAT IF WE DON'T FIND ALLIES?

WE WILL, RHUS.

CADADOR HAS POWER, BUT MERIDIAN HAS STRENGTH *AND* PATIENCE.

THEY'LL COME TO RUE THE DAY.

TAKE THIS, JAD.

I KNOW WHAT THEY PACKED YOUR SHIP WITH, AND IT'S FORTIFYING, BUT NOTHING SPECIAL.

THANKS...

...MOM.

Oh, *YOU!*

BE *CAREFUL* THERE IN CADADOR! FIND HER QUICKLY AND GET AWAY JUST AS FAST! NOW, *GO!*

WAIT! JAD, DON'T LEAVE BEFORE WE...

...GET OUR CHANCE TO WISH YOU GOOD JOURNEY!

IT'S SO BRAVE...

...YOU GOING OFF ALONE TO... RESCUE SEPHIE.

I HAVE TO BE BRAVE.

IT'LL BE DANGEROUS.

IF THE SOLDIERS OF CADADOR CATCH ME --

JAD...

YA!!!!

THERE'S ONE NOW...

...AND YOU'RE HIS PRISONER!

DID I INTERRUPT?

I JUST CAME BY TO REMIND YOU TO STAY OUT OF TROUBLE IN CAPADOR.

MEET UP WITH US AT RING CITY AS SOON AS YOU CAN.

SURE, DAD...

HEE HEE HEE HEEHEE HEEHEE HEE HEE HEE

IF YOU CAN'T FIND HER, LEAVE A MESSAGE AND MOVE ON.

JAD --

-- DON'T PUT YOURSELF IN UNNECESSARY DANGER...

...PLEASE...

...BECAUSE NO ONE COULD REPLACE YOU.

I'LL BE CAREFUL, DAD.

"GATHER AROUND, EVERYONE...

"I'M NOT MUCH OF AN ORATOR, BUT SOME WORDS NEED TO BE SAID.

"IT'S TIME TO GREET OUR FUTURE.

"AS WE LEAVE MERIDIAN, WE MUST BE OPEN TO THE POSSIBILITY THAT OUR RETURN MAY COME A FAR TIME FROM NOW.

"BUT, ALTHOUGH WE ARE LEAVING THE *LAND* OF MERIDIAN BEHIND...

"...NO MATTER WHERE THIS WIND TAKES US, NO MATTER HOW FAR OR HOW LONG...

"...AS LONG AS WE CARRY HER *ESSENCE* WITHIN US...

...WE WILL ALWAYS BE THE PEOPLE OF MERIDIAN.

GJOURNEY, JAD!

HURRY BACK TO US!

WELL SAID.

AAAH!

IT'S
HEALTHY?

LAST NIGHT, AS YOU WERE SUFFERING THROUGH THE TRAUMA OF YOUR...LANDFALL...

...I UNDERSTOOD YOU TO SAY YOU WERE THE MINISTER OF MERIDIAN.

BUT I'VE *MET* TUROS.

I'M HIS DAUGHTER.

MY FATHER... DIED, VERY RECENTLY.

I *AM* MINISTER NOW.

Maraya, the Minister of Akasia, was so welcoming. The people were all so kind. They made me want to stay there forever.

The city seemed as warm as the dyes Akasia is known for...

...I know better now.

EEYEW.

SO...A SHIP FROM MERIDIAN BROUGHT YOU HERE?

NO... A SHIP FROM CAPADOR. I WAS STAYING WITH MY UNCLE ILAHN, BUT I'M ON MY WAY HOME NOW.

I'VE NEVER BEEN TO A SURFACE CITY BEFORE.

LITTLE COMMERCE HAPPENS HERE-- WE'RE DEPENDENT ON THE TRADE SHIPS.

IS YOUR UNCLE ILAHN THE SAME ILAHN WHO IS MINISTER OF CAPADOR?

THEN YOU MUST HAVE A FULL TOUR.

WEAVER'S GUILD...

...WE'RE NOT RICH LIKE CAPADOR, BUT OUR DYES KEEP US PROSPEROUS IN OUR OWN WAY.

6.1

YES, THAT'S HIM.

Hmmmm...

AS YOU KNOW, THE SURFACE IS MORE TREACHEROUS THAN THE SKY CITIES, BUT WE OF AKASIA HAVE FORGED A BALANCE BETWEEN DANGER AND VALUE.

WE FLOAT LIKE YOUR CITIES, BUT NOT ON ROCKS-- WE KEEP OUR ANCIENT CONNECTION TO THE GROUND.

THE CATACLYSM MAY HAVE POISONED THE LAND, BUT THOSE SAME TOXINS ACT AS MORPANTS FOR OUR DYES.

ISN'T IT DANGEROUS?

SOMEWHAT, BUT ALL WORK POSES SOME DANGER.

THE REWARDS ARE MANY-- SINCE OUR OWN BIRTH RATES ARE LOW, WE ARE EVEN ABLE TO TAKE IN FOUNDLING CHILDREN FROM ALL OVER DEMETRIA!

MY FAMILY DOES THAT. WE'VE ALWAYS GIVEN A HOME TO...

...ORPHANS.

When we talked about the orphans, my stomach lurched.

Papa's death meant that word now included me.

TRADE WITH THE LOGGERS TO THE EAST NETS US RAW LUMBER.

OUR WOODWORKERS DO THE LOVELY INLAY WORK WE'RE KNOWN FOR *AND* OVERSEE THE PERPETUAL RECONSTRUCTION OF AKASIA.

I KNOW YOU MUST BE EAGER TO RETURN TO CADAPOR.

YOUR UNCLE MISSES YOU, NO?

I DON'T THINK SO. HE KNEW I WAS GOING HOME.

BY NOW, HE KNOWS I'M...

...SAFE.

RECONSTRUCTION, YOU SAID?

CONSTANT. THE GROUND PREMATURELY AGES THE WOOD, SO WE MUST KEEP BUILDING NEW ZONES WHILE PREPARING TO ABANDON OTHERS.

WE MAKE SURE THERE IS ALWAYS A HOME FOR EVERY AKASIAN. MOST OF OUR CITIZENS WORKED IN THE DYE FACTORIES...

Cadador is cold despite its riches.

Akasia has a humble beauty, but the STENCH...

I was curious about her city, but so lonely for Meridian.

THERE'S NO WAY TO BALANCE THE EQUATION? BUILD STRUCTURES THAT WITHSTAND THE EROSION?

THE DECAYING ZONES ARE NOT BEAUTIFUL, BUT IT'S MORE COST-EFFICIENT TO KEEP BUILDING THAN TO SHORE UP THE PARTS THAT HAVE DECAYED.

WE MUST ALWAYS MOVE FORWARD AND ABANDON THE PAST.

AKASIA PALES NEXT TO CAPADOR, BUT IT IS OUR HOME, AND THE MINISTER OF MERIDIAN IS WELCOME TO STAY HERE FOR AS LONG AS IT TAKES HER TO REST FROM HER GRUELING JOURNEY.

PLEASE, THINK OF THIS AS YOUR HOME.

THANK YOU. THAT'S SO KIND.

HOW COULD WE DO LESS FOR A SPECIAL VISITOR FROM...

6.3

"...CADADOR?"

JAD! SO, IT'S THE LITTLE TAKARTY!

AVY, DON'T CALL ME --

THE CADADORS HAVE TAKEN OVER MERIDIAN AND EVERYBODY'S GONE TO GROUND?

AVY, ARE YOU *IMPLYING* THAT I WOULD KNOW *ANYTHING* ABOUT *ANY* ESCAPE PLAN?

SO, WHAT'S THE NEWS FROM HOME? I HEAR IT'S BAD.

HEY, JADLING, WELCOME TO CADADOR PORT!

Oh, YEAH, RIGHT. YOUR PA'S *ONLY* THE CLOSEST THING WE'VE GOT TO A GENERAL THERE.

SNIP!

YOU MAY BE YOUNG, BUT YOU'RE NOT STUPID.

SPILL.

THE COUNCIL AND MOST EVERYBODY WHO WANTED ARE MOVING ON, LEAVING MERIDIAN...

I'M HERE TO GET SEPHIE AND BRING HER ALONG.

LEAVING MERIDIAN?

IT'S THAT BAD?

JAD, MY CONTRACT'S UP SOON AND I WAS WANTING TO GO HOME...

I'M SORRY, AVY. IT'S NOT A GOOD IDEA RIGHT NOW.

YOU COULD MEET US AT--

SHHH! WALLS HAVE EARS.

WATCH YOUR BACK AND YOUR MOUTH WHILE YOU'RE IN CAPADOR, JAD.

THEY THINK ILAHN'S A HERO HERE.

THIS ROUTE COMES OUT TOPSIDE.

KEEP TO THE SHADOWS, JADLING. WE STAND OUT IN THIS BIG CITY.

I'LL KEEP AN EYE ON YOUR SKYSHIP-- KEEP IT READY TO LEAVE WHEN YOU GET BACK.

GOOD LUCK!

AVY!

ALL I'VE GOT TO DO IS SNEAK ONTO ILAHN'S PRIVATE ISLAND...

"...HOW HARD COULD THAT BE?"

YES, LOROSI?

MINISTER ILAHN, I MAY HAVE --

I HAVE --

MAY I HAVE --?

THE POINT, LOROSI.

COME TO IT QUICKLY.

THE WOMAN I SPOKE TO YOU OF YESTERDAY?

SHE'S HERE NOW...

...BUT I WILL OF COURSE SEND HER AWAY.

NOT A GOOD TIME.

ABSOLUTELY NOT! SEND HER IN.

I KEEP MY WORD AND MY APPOINTMENTS.

GOOD.

I ADMIRE THAT IN MY TEACHERS.

6.7

6.8

"...ALTHOUGH THE HEIR IS NOT AS LOST AS HE IMAGINES."

WHY ARE THEY RUNNING?

Oh, NO. TO HIGH GROUND! *QUICKLY!*

CELANAUG!

THEY'RE FERAL TOXIN-DWELLERS -- BUT IT'S DAYLIGHT!

HURRY -- WE MUST STAY TO THE GOOD AREAS!

NO, SEPHIE -- *THIS* WAY.

BUT, LOOK!

Realization of the danger posed by the monsters of Akasia reached my brain too late...

...my heart had already gone out to the child caught in its path.

6.9

I'd never been fearful.

Papa even described me as reckless...

SEPHIE, NO!

WE CAN'T LOSE YOU!

YOU WON'T!

...but the feeling that hit me, seeing that boy in danger...

KRA CRAK

...the sudden fire inside me came from someplace new...

JUMP!

...and there was NOTHING that was going to stop me from saving him!

Suddenly, I was more than Sephie! I was a mythic goddess of protection!

While I was filled with life and strength, no other lives would be lost!

KERAKK

No matter what kind of monsters I had to face.

For an instant, I thought I'd reached a perfect understanding of why I'd been given the sign of power...

KERAAAK

...a vision that slipped out of my head as the decaying boards under my feet gave way...

AAAH!

KRUNCH

...and I felt my confidence drop down past my feet into the pit.

6.11

Until I spotted the celahawg's cold eyes below...

No snarly-faced toxin-licker was going to stop ME!

This time, when I MADE it happen, I was AWARE of the power coming from me...

...I could feel the fibers repairing themselves...

...as I FORCED it all whole again!

The monster couldn't break through good wood...

...so I poured everything I had inside into creating an avenue of escape...

...one step ahead of the monster.

HOW MANY? THREE?

AND IN DAYLIGHT...

THEY'RE GETTING BOLDER.

The attack left me thrilled at the potential of my new power, and ready to sleep for a week.

THANK YOU, BUT WHY? HOW?

I -- *huh* --

...JUST DID -- *huh*...

...*huh*...

...WHAT WAS RIGHT TO DO.

huh

huh

huh

It also left me feeling I'd grown two heads and a furry tail, the way they all STARED.

RING CITY IN SIGHT! WE'LL MAKE PORT WITHIN THE HOUR.

LOOKS LIKE THEY'RE SENDING OUT A GREETER SHIP...

...WITH ITS SAILS SET FOR MAXIMUM SPEED.

THEY'RE IN A DARNED HURRY...

...HOPE IT ISN'T BAD NEWS.

HULLO, PLAINSAILS!

YOU'RE FROM MERIDIAN, RIGHT?

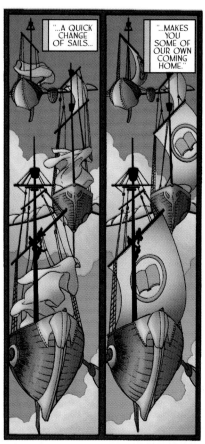

"...A QUICK CHANGE OF SAILS...

"...MAKES YOU SOME OF OUR OWN COMING HOME."

BUT... WE'RE FROM *MERIDIAN!* WE DON'T MARK OUR SAILS....

OUR SAILS ARE STILL UNMARKED, LAD! THEY'RE JUST BEING HIDDEN SO OUR *STERNS* STAY UNMARKED ALSO!

BUT, MIRA, IT'S-- *WRONG!*

SOMETIMES THE WORLD GOES WRONG, ENOS.

MAYBE RIGHT NOW WE MUST HIDE WHO WE ARE...

...BUT THAT DOESN'T MEAN WE'LL *FORGET.*

THE GIRL LET THINGS SLIP IN HER DELIRIUM LAST NIGHT.

NO SHIP BROUGHT HER --

-- SEPHIE OF MERIDIAN FELL FROM THE AIR AND *DID NOT DIE.*

THIS WAS WITNESSED BY ILAHN'S SOLDIERS, SO ILAHN MUST BELIEVE HER DEAD.

DOES THAT HAVE SOMETHING TO DO WITH THIS REJUVENATION?

YES.

SHE DID IT.

YOU SAW WHAT SHE DID AGAINST THE CELANAUG.

I BROUGHT YOU OUT HERE TO ADVISE ME IN A DECISION:

DO WE ENTICE SEPHIE TO STAY?

KEEP THE GIRL IN AKASIA, HIDDEN, OR SEND A MESSENGER TO CADADOR?

KEEP HER!

IF ILAHN BELIEVES HER DEAD, HE'LL NEVER LOOK FOR HER HERE!

WE SIMPLY... FAIL TO NOTIFY.

CHEATING ILAHN'S A DANGER.

IF HIS SPIES EVER DISCOVER HER, TRADE SHIPS COULD SKIP OUR PORT.

DON'T FORGET HIS BLOCKADE OF SEGEN OR WHAT HE'S THREATENING TO DO TO TORBEL...

...LET IT *FALL.*

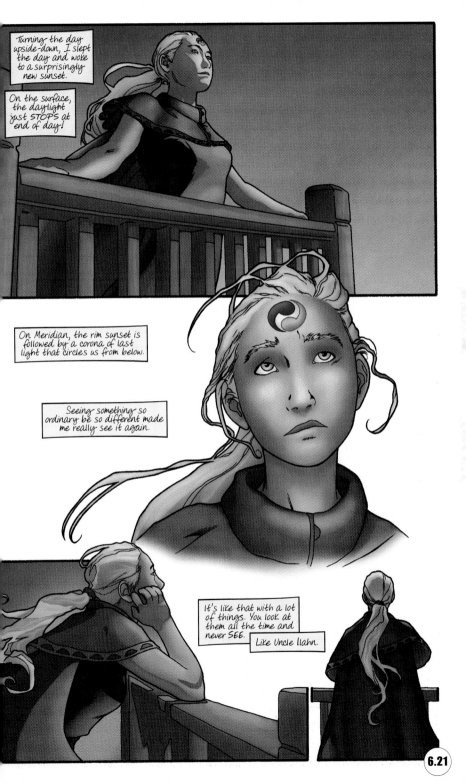

Turning the day upside-down, I slept the day and woke to a surprisingly new sunset.

On the surface, the daylight just STOPS at end of day!

On Meridian, the rim sunset is followed by a corona of last light that circles us from below.

Seeing something so ordinary be so different made me really see it again.

It's like that with a lot of things. You look at them all the time and never SEE.

Like Uncle Ilahn.

6.21

Sunset had never been more to me than a cue to go home, but that night it became a living symbol of my promise to Meridian.

Ilahn of Cadador would NOT destroy my island.

I'd do something good for the people of Akasia to repay them for their kindness, but then it was time for me to go home...

...and start a war.

The economy of Akasia revolves around a cycle of decay.

They rebuild the city at one end and abandon the other as ground toxins eat it away.

It's a business decision: construction is cheaper than prevention...

...and Akasia is poor.

Growing up on Meridian, I didn't know what kind of disease "poor" was, only that surface people had it.

When they earned enough to recover, they moved up to the sky cities.

I never joined Papa on journeys to the surface...

...I was afraid I'd catch the disease.

And now, I was its cure.

Reaching out with my fingers I could feel what needed to be fixed and find the power to make it right.

The mark on my head gave me a gift.

Papa's love taught me to share.

Although he'd wink and point out that creating goodwill IS good business.

...WHAT ARE YOU STANDING ON?

STANDING --
AAAAH!

OH! AAAAH! NOOO!

SEPHIE!

SPLUUUTCH

...THAT'S NOT HOW WE DID IT ON MERIDIAN.

BUT YOU'RE NOT ON MERIDIAN...

...YOU'RE IN *RING CITY* NOW.

AND WE HAVE OUR OWN WAYS OF COAXING WORN EQUIPMENT BACK INTO SERVICE.

IF YOU'D JUST SERVICE YOUR MACHINES MORE FAITHFULLY, YOU'D SEE BETTER SERVICE FROM THEM!

GENTLEMEN!

GENTLEWOMEN! SORRY TO INTERRUPT. I'M MINISTER ODWIN. WELCOME TO RING CITY!

I'M SORRY WE HAD TO HUSTLE YOU ALL INTO HERE, BUT YOU UNDERSTAND THE *SITUATION* WITH CADADOR.

TAKARTY, CAN I SPEAK WITH YOU...

...PRIVATELY?

JON, I RECOGNIZE THAT YOU AND YOURS HAVE HAD TO GIVE UP EVERYTHING TO LEAVE MERIDIAN...

...AND I DON'T WANT TO ADD WEIGHT TO YOUR BURDEN...

...BUT I'VE A RESPONSIBILITY TO MY CITYMATES TO ASK YOU THIS:

WHAT ARE YOUR PLANS, JON? ARE YOU GOING TO *STAY* IN RING CITY?

YOU'RE ALL WELCOME TO LIVE HERE -- WE'VE PLENTY OF ROOM -- BUT WE CAN'T CONTINUE TO HIDE YOU AWAY.

THERE'S BOUND TO BE A SLIP.

WE'LL PROTECT YOU FOR AS LONG AS POSSIBLE, BUT I HAVE TO WATCH OVER OUR CITY'S SECURITY...

"...BECAUSE CADADORIAN SOLDIERS LURK EVERYWHERE."

7.9

7.11

I MYSELF WAS NOT BORN ON CADADOR.

I GAINED MINISTERSHIP OF THE ISLAND THROUGH MARRIAGE.

MY WIFE... WAS A FRAIL WOMAN.

HER MOTHER WAS MINISTER BEFORE ME. SHE BROKERED OUR MARRIAGE SHORTLY BEFORE HER OWN DEATH.

MY WIFE DIED CHILDLESS. I HAD GREAT HOPES THAT SEPHIE WOULD BE MY HEIR...

...BUT HER MISADVENTURE HAS ENSURED THAT IT WILL NEVER COME TO PASS.

YOU ARE RIGHT. I LACK AN HEIR.

WHOEVER I NAME WILL GAIN CONTROL OF DEMETRIA AFTER ME.

BUT NOT WITHOUT *EARNING* IT. AS YOU WELL KNOW...

...THERE ARE MANY WAYS TO DO BUSINESS.

AND MANY ROADS TO POWER.

AND IT WOULD APPEAR THAT YOU'VE TROD THEM ALL, YOUNG LADY.

...BUT I TRANSCEND THE SENSATION...

...BECAUSE I HAVE BECOME ONE WITH *DESTRUCTION*...

...AND DESTRUCTION ENDS ALL PAIN.

BUT NOT *ALL* FEELING?

NO.

NOK NOK

MINISTER ILAHN?

THERE'S A MESSENGER FROM *AKASIA*. NEWS ABOUT--

IT'S A *PERSONAL* MESSAGE.

BEFORE YOU LEAVE US, SEPHIE... ...THERE'S STILL A PART OF AKASIA YOU HAVEN'T SEEN.

YOU'VE SEEN OUR CRAFTS. LET ME GIVE YOU A TOUR OF OUR INDUSTRY.

I'D LIKE THAT!

GUARD, PASS ON A MESSAGE FOR ME...

YES, MY MINISTER.

I'M ALWAYS CURIOUS TO SEE HOW OTHER CITIES WORK.

THIS IS WHERE YOUR DYES ARE PROCESSED?

YES, AND WE'RE RATHER PROUD OF THE INNOVATIVE WAY WE KEEP IT COST-EFFICIENT...

7.21

THEY'RE EARNING THE RIGHT TO BE CITIZENS.

AS MOST OF US DID BEFORE THEM.

I CAN'T BELIEVE YOU WOULD DO THIS!

WHAT ARE YOU DOING TO ME?

CLANGK

NO! YOU CAN'T LOCK ME IN HERE!

I WON'T LET YOU!

BUT -- IT'S NOT WORKING!

IT'S NOT DOING ANYTHING!

NOOO...

I'M SO SORRY, SEPHIE.

BUT MY CONCERNS ARE GREATER THAN THE WELL-BEING OF ONE CHILD.

YOU ARE A RESOURCE WE NEED.

YOUR GIFT WILL HELP AKASIA.

I HAVE TO KEEP YOU HERE.

AS A FELLOW MINISTER, I KNOW YOU'LL UNDERSTAND.

The cover is the single most important piece of artwork produced for any issue. It must communicate not only the story's essence, but also be engaging enough to attract attention on a crowded comic rack. Covers for MERIDIAN, a book that depends more upon careful character development than steroid-enhanced action, have the added obstacle of usually steering away from the fight scenes that dominate so many comic covers.

Original series artist Josh Middleton designed the world of Demetria as a fairy-tale environment, a setting that needed to be conveyed through cover images like issue #1's montage piece. Ensuing covers offered iconic images of Sephie and her Uncle Ilahn. Issue #3's cover shows a seated Ilahn holding a globe. According to writer Barbara Kesel, "He's holding it but also destroying it, showing how much of a cold creature he is. And that was a great contrast to the cover of #4, where we go from Ilahn's cold villainy to the bright heroism of Sephie."

Issue #7 marked the first cover from Steve McNiven, who would shortly take over drawing the book on a monthly basis and truly make MERIDIAN his own. McNiven's style and confidence have both matured since he drew his "mirror image" cover.

"When I look at it now there are a lot of things I'd definitely change, but I do think it works in establishing the relationship between Ilahn and Reesha," McNiven said. "At the time I didn't know how long I'd be on MERIDIAN. But I was determined to have some fun. I think I've come a long way, that's for sure."

Here's another look at MERIDIAN's first seven covers:

COVER GALLERY

CROSSGEN COMICS®
GRAPHIC NOVELS

COMING SOON:
SIGIL vol. 4: HOSTAGE PLANET and ROUTE 666 vol. 1: HIGHWAY OF HORROR